FLIGHT TEST LAB
HELICOPTERS

by Paul Beck

Silver Dolphin
San Diego, California

To my father

Silver Dolphin
Silver Dolphin Books
An imprint of the Advantage Publishers Group
5880 Oberlin Drive, San Diego, CA 92121-4794
www.silverdolphinbooks.com

Text copyright © 2003 by becker&mayer!

Flight Test Lab: Helicopters is produced by becker&mayer!,
Bellevue, Washington
www.beckermayer.com

If you have questions or comments about this product, send e-mail to
infobm@beckermayer.com.

ISBN 1-59223-025-3

Produced, manufactured, and assembled in China.

3 4 5 6 7 09 08 07 06 05

04377

Edited by Ben Grossblatt
Art direction and design by Scott Westgard & Andrew Hess
Casewrap design by Scott Westgard
Illustrated by Joshua Beach (casewrap, pages 1–3, 24–27, 32),
Harry Whitver (pages 4–5), Charles Floyd (pages 6–9),
John Laidlaw (pages 6, 7, 28–31), Michael Ingrassia (pages 10–11),
and Stephan Kuhn (pages 12–23)
Toy development by Mark Byrnes
Production management by Jennifer Marx
Facts checked by Melody Moss
Special thanks to Andrew Nash for the *Albatross* image
and to Alissa Lenz.

Table of Contents

PREPARE FOR LIFTOFF

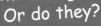

From fighting deadly forest fires to rescuing troops behind enemy lines, helicopters perform incredible feats. Master flight theory, stay on top of the latest technology, and discover how these mechanical marvels work.

This Flight Test Lab includes all the parts—including a launcher—to assemble your own flying helicopters: a firefighting helicopter, a police copter, a military chopper, and a rescue helicopter. Or mix and match the parts to create your own designs.

First things first: What is a helicopter? A helicopter is an aircraft, one that looks different from an airplane and flies differently, too. What makes the difference? Simple. Helicopters don't have wings.

Or do they?

Anatomy of a Helicopter

The **main rotor** lifts the helicopter into the air and moves it forward, backward, or sideways.

Some helicopters have a single, main rotor, while others have two. The rotors on most tandem-rotor (two-rotor) helicopters are at the front and back ends, but some have a rotor on each side of the fuselage. Some even have two stacked rotors!

The **pitch control rods** push up and pull down to change the pitch, or angle, of the rotor blades. Changing the pitch of the blades controls the helicopter's flight.

The **cabin** may have different purposes, depending on what job the helicopter does. It can hold passengers, cargo, medical beds and equipment, weapons, or a combination of any of those things.

The **cockpit** is where the pilot and copilot sit. If the helicopter is built to hold only one or two people, this is the only cabin.

It's All a Blur
Helicopter rotors spin so fast that the blades blur together and look like one large disk. In fact, helicopter pilots and engineers find it useful to talk about the spinning rotor as if it were a single, disk-shaped wing called the rotor disk.

The **fuselage** (FEW-suh-laj) is the body of the helicopter.

Actually, helicopters do have wings. Instead of fixed (nonmoving) wings like the ones on an airplane, a helicopter has a spinning wing called a rotor. A rotor is made up of two or more blades attached to a hub. If you look carefully at a helicopter's rotor blades, you'll see that each one is shaped like a long, narrow wing.

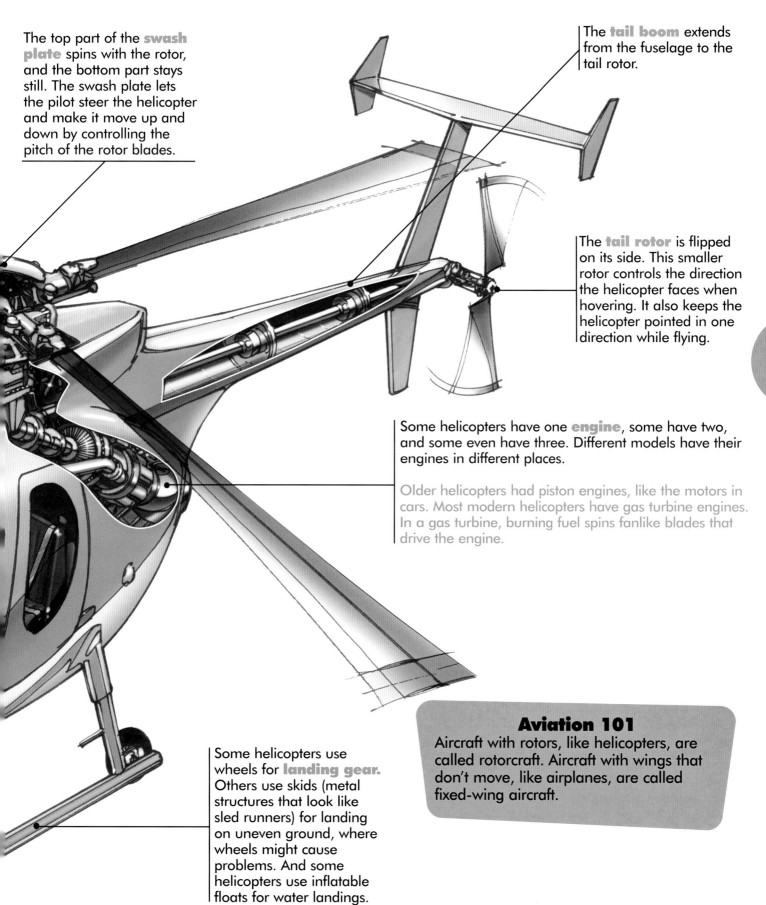

The top part of the **swash plate** spins with the rotor, and the bottom part stays still. The swash plate lets the pilot steer the helicopter and make it move up and down by controlling the pitch of the rotor blades.

The **tail boom** extends from the fuselage to the tail rotor.

The **tail rotor** is flipped on its side. This smaller rotor controls the direction the helicopter faces when hovering. It also keeps the helicopter pointed in one direction while flying.

Some helicopters have one **engine**, some have two, and some even have three. Different models have their engines in different places.

Older helicopters had piston engines, like the motors in cars. Most modern helicopters have gas turbine engines. In a gas turbine, burning fuel spins fanlike blades that drive the engine.

Some helicopters use wheels for **landing gear.** Others use skids (metal structures that look like sled runners) for landing on uneven ground, where wheels might cause problems. And some helicopters use inflatable floats for water landings.

Aviation 101
Aircraft with rotors, like helicopters, are called rotorcraft. Aircraft with wings that don't move, like airplanes, are called fixed-wing aircraft.

Foundations of Flight

A helicopter, and anything else that flies—airplane, bird, or blimp—
has to balance four forces to stay up in the air.

FOUR FORCES OF FLIGHT

The forces of flight oppose, or work against, each other in pairs.

Lift and gravity are opposites. If lift is greater than gravity, the helicopter rises. If lift is less, the helicopter drops. If lift and gravity are equal, the helicopter stays at one altitude.

Thrust and drag are opposites. If thrust is greater than drag, the helicopter speeds up. If thrust is less, it slows down. If thrust and drag are equal, the helicopter moves at a steady speed.

Thrust is the force that moves the helicopter forward, sideways, or backward. A helicopter's thrust comes from its rotor.

Gravity is the force that pulls everything on earth—including helicopters—toward the ground. We feel gravity as weight.

SPECIAL HELICOPTER FORCES

When it flies, a helicopter has to deal with some extra forces that other aircraft don't. These extra forces come from its spinning rotor.

ROTOR DRAG

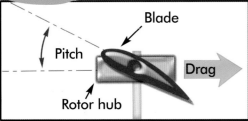

lower pitch = less drag   *higher pitch = more drag*

Not only is there drag on the aircraft as it flies against the air, but there's also drag on each rotor blade as it spins through the air. When a blade's pitch increases, it meets the air at a steeper angle, and there's more drag. When that happens, the engine has to put out more power so the rotor doesn't slow down. (If the rotor slows down, the helicopter loses lift.)

TORQUE

Torque (pronounced "tork") is twisting force. To see how torque affects a helicopter, try an experiment. Sit in an office chair that swivels. Hold your arms out to one side. Now rotate them across the front of your body to the other side. Do you notice your hips turning in the opposite direction?

Lift is the force that raises the helicopter into the air and keeps it there. A helicopter's lift comes from its rotor.

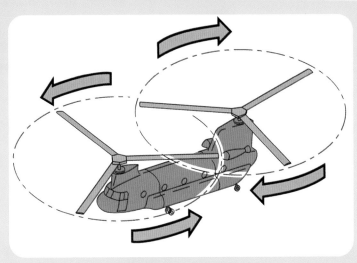

Double Rotors

Helicopters with two main rotors, like the U.S. Army's Chinook, don't have tail rotors. Instead, the main rotors turn in opposite directions. The torque reaction from each rotor acts against the reaction from the other.

The rotors are synchronized so that the blades mesh with each other instead of colliding.

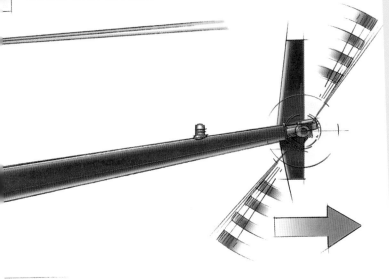

Drag is a force that slows the helicopter down. Drag is also called air resistance. A helicopter has to push its way through the air, and the air flowing against it slows the helicopter down.

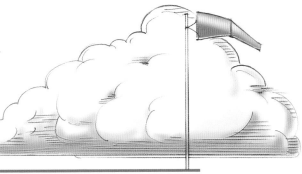

You've twisted your way to an important law of physics: Newton's third law of motion, discovered by the English scientist Isaac Newton. Newton's third law says: "For every action, there is an equal and opposite reaction."

Here's what that means for your body and a helicopter:

Action: Your muscles' torque twists your arms across your body.
Reaction: Your hips twist in the opposite direction.

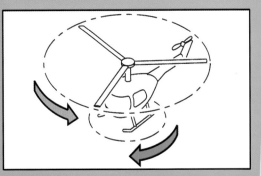

Action: The engine's torque twists the rotor in one direction.
Reaction: The helicopter twists in the opposite direction. That's called the torque reaction.

When the rotor turns counterclockwise, torque makes the fuselage turn clockwise. That's why helicopters have tail—or antitorque—rotors. They act against torque by creating a force to turn the copter counterclockwise. The spinning forces cancel each other out, and the helicopter stays straight.

Airfoils and Helicopters

You know that the spinning rotor is what keeps a helicopter in the air. But how does it work? The secret is in the shape of the rotor blades and the way they move through the air.

ALL ABOUT AIRFOILS

A helicopter rotor blade (and the typical airplane wing, too) is called an airfoil. An airfoil's shape is very important.

The air flows over the surface of the blade and is turned downward. The air "sticks" to the blade as the blade moves through it. This is called the Coanda effect, named for the Romanian scientist Henri Coanda. Coanda discovered that when a fluid, like air, flows along a curved surface, it follows the contour of that surface.

Air Is a Fluid?

When we talk about a fluid, we usually mean a liquid, like water. But to scientists, a fluid is any substance with molecules that are free to move around. That means both liquids and gases (like air) are fluids. Liquids and gases act alike in many ways. The study of how they behave is called fluid dynamics.

When viewed from above, the typical helicopter's main rotor spins in a counterclockwise direction (see the red arrows in the diagram below). As the blades spin, air flows over and under the blades in a clockwise direction (the blue and green arrows).

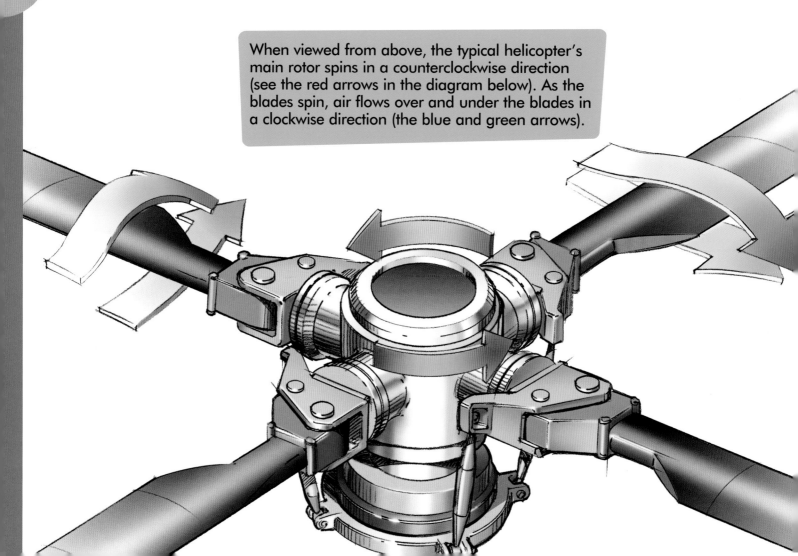

The flow of air around the blade creates the lift. Engineers need very complicated math equations to explain how lift happens, but there are two ways you can think of it:

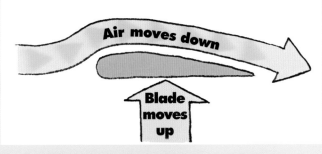

The Newton Explanation

Remember Newton's third law of motion? "For every action, there is an equal and opposite reaction." The air flowing across the blade gets turned downward as it flows. That's the action. Because of that, the blade moves upward. That's the reaction, and that's lift!

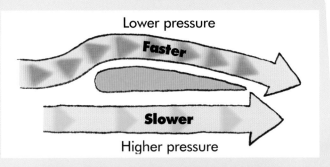

The Bernoulli Explanation

The Swiss scientist Daniel Bernoulli discovered that the pressure of a fluid depends on how fast the fluid is moving.

A faster-moving fluid has a lower pressure than a slower-moving one. Tests show that the air flowing along the top of the blade moves faster than the air flowing along the bottom, so the pressure on top is lower and the pressure on the bottom is higher. The higher pressure on the bottom pushes the blade upward, and that's lift!

ANGLES AND AIRFOILS

The shape of an airfoil is important, but so is the angle at which it meets the air. Imagine that you could stand on a helicopter's rotor blade. As the blade moved through the air, you would feel a strong wind blowing in your face. The direction that "wind" blows is called the relative airflow.

The angle between the blade and the relative airflow is called the angle of attack. The steeper the angle of attack, the greater the amount of lift.

Pitch and Angle of Attack

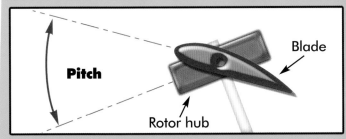

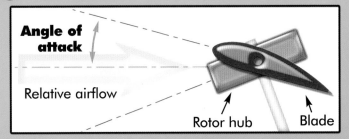

A rotor blade's pitch and angle of attack are related, but they're not the same thing. The pitch is the angle between the blade and the rotor hub. Changing the pitch changes the angle of attack, but the angle of attack also depends on wind direction and the tilt of the rotor disk.

If the angle of attack gets too large, the air doesn't flow smoothly around the blade. Instead, it becomes turbulent, or rough, like rapids in a river. When that happens, the airfoil loses all of its lift. That's called a stall.

In the Pilot's Seat

Helicopter pilots need quick eyes, careful hands, and steady nerves. They need to keep track of gauges and dials for information about the helicopter's flight: speed, direction, and position. By adjusting the controls, a pilot tells the parts of the helicopter what to do, and that makes the helicopter fly where and how the pilot wants.

Changing Course

When the rotor disk is tilted, the helicopter moves in a different direction. The helicopter moves in the direction the rotor shaft points. To tilt the rotor disk, the pilot moves the cyclic control.

Adjusting the cyclic control causes each rotor blade's pitch to change as it spins. When the cyclic control is moved forward, the changing pitches of the blades cause the rotor disk to point forward and the helicopter moves forward.

The same thing happens when the pilot moves the cyclic control backward or to the side: each blade's pitch changes as it spins and the effect is a tilted rotor disk.

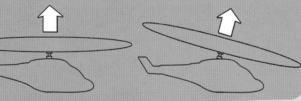

The **vertical speed indicator** shows how fast the helicopter is rising or descending.

The **attitude indicator** (also called the artificial horizon) shows how much the helicopter's fuselage is tilted, both front-to-back (called pitch) and sideways (called roll).

Pushing the **antitorque pedals** changes the direction the helicopter points. Pushing one pedal increases the pitch of the tail rotor blades. Pushing the other decreases the pitch.

When the pitch of the tail rotor blades increases, the tail rotor produces more torque than the main rotor and the helicopter's fuselage swivels counterclockwise. When the pitch of the tail rotor blades decreases, the tail rotor produces less torque and the fuselage swivels clockwise.

This swiveling motion is called yaw, so these pedals are sometimes called yaw pedals.

The helicopter's altitude, or height above sea level, is displayed on the **altimeter** (al-TIM-uh-ter). The altimeter has two hands, like a clock. The short hand shows thousands of feet above sea level, and the long hand shows hundreds.

Cockpit Controls and What They Do

Cockpit Control	Effect	Motion
Collective pitch lever	Changes pitch of all main rotor blades at the same time	Up and down
Cyclic control	Changes pitch of each of the main rotor blades as it spins	Forward, backward, sideways
Antitorque pedals	Change pitch of tail rotor blades	Helicopter swivels, points in different direction

The **airspeed indicator** shows how fast the helicopter is moving.

The **tachometer** (tack-AH-muh-ter) shows the number of revolutions per minute (rpm) of the rotor and the engine. The tachometer also has two hands. One shows the rotor rpm and the other shows the engine rpm.

The **cyclic control** moves like the joystick for a video game. It changes the pitch of each rotor blade in a cycle, moving from high pitch to low and back again as the rotor spins.

Making adjustments to the **trim control** keeps the helicopter flying straight and level.

Cargo release switch

Direction indicator

Manifold pressure indicator

The **collective pitch lever** moves up and down and changes the pitch of all the rotor blades at the same time. Pulling the lever up increases the pitch, and pushing it down decreases the pitch.

More pitch means more lift. To make the helicopter go up, the pilot pulls up on the collective pitch lever. To make the helicopter go down, the pilot moves the lever down.

Helicopters have a **throttle** at the end of the collective pitch lever. The pilot twists the handle to increase or decrease the speed of the engine.

Flying Tankers

Special helicopters can fight fires almost anywhere. In the wilderness, they don't need roads or runways. In the city, they don't get slowed down by traffic. Helicopters can refill their tanks from the air, so they don't lose any time landing for more water.

FIRE!

A forest fire is attacking the mountain. Brilliant patches of orange flame twist in billows of thick smoke. A house stands just uphill from the fire. The residents escaped minutes before, knowing that soon their house and all their belongings could be destroyed.

A Helitanker zooms overhead like a giant insect. It slows as it reaches the fire. Moving carefully above the line of the advancing flames, the pilot opens the tank doors and 2,500 gallons of water spill from the belly of the aircraft onto the burning trees below. Steam rolls up as a large area of flames goes out.

The helicopter turns and flies back to the lake at the base of the mountain. It hovers low as its hanging snorkel sucks water into the tank.

Less than a minute later the tank is full and the copter heads back up the mountain. The firefighters are winning—the flames have slowed and the house will be saved.

The six-bladed **main rotor** measures 72 feet across. Usually, the rotors of helicopters that lift a lot of weight have more blades than the rotors of lighter helicopters. The blade load is the amount of the helicopter's weight that each blade has to hold up in the air. If there are more blades, the blade load for each individual blade is less.

The **water tank** holds up to 2,500 gallons of water or fire-retardant chemicals. (That's about what 50 bathtubs can hold!)

A separate tank can hold firefighting foam to be mixed in with the water. Foam helps the water cover more area and extinguish flames better.

Heavy Lifters

Helitankers have to be able to lift a lot of weight. A full tank of water weighs 20,000 pounds, as much as six medium-sized cars! This aircraft is one version of a type of helicopter called a sky crane. Notice how the cockpit, fuselage, and landing gear could fit over the top of a large object like a shipping container or even a truck. The lifting power of a sky crane lets it move heavy objects in and out of places where it would be very hard to bring a truck or crane.

Other Sky Crane Jobs
- Hydroseeding, or dropping a liquid mix of fertilizer and seeds to plant grass and other vegetation over a large area
- Carrying construction materials and heavy equipment into wilderness locations
- Placing ski lift, tram, and power poles
- Lifting cut timber from logging areas

The **cockpit** has room for two pilots and an extra person. Most of the helicopter's carrying space is taken up by the water tank.

The **doors** on the bottom of the tank are computer-controlled, to let the pilot choose how much area to cover with the water.

The hanging **snorkel** fills the tank while the copter hovers over a source of water. The snorkel works in water as shallow as 18 inches! A pump slurps up water so quickly that it can fill up the whole tank in 45 seconds.

The **water cannon** lets the copter fight fires in tall buildings. The water cannon can spray out 300 gallons of water per minute. With a full tank of water, it can keep spraying for eight minutes before the tank has to be refilled.

Military Choppers

All branches of the military use helicopters—like the Black Hawk shown below—for fighting in battles, moving people and equipment, search and rescue, medical evacuations, and scouting out territory.

Attack helicopters carry many **weapons** for self-defense.

The Black Hawk helicopter is fitted with machine guns inside the doors on both sides of the cabin. The helicopter can also carry rockets and laser-guided missiles.

MISSION AT MIDNIGHT

The night is black and moonless. The chopper flies only a few feet above the tops of the trees, hugging the dips and rises of the ground to avoid being spotted by the enemy.

The helicopter is dark. The pilot and crew wear night-vision goggles that let them navigate and see dials and gauges that would be nearly invisible without them. In the cabin, the crew chief crouches by the door gun, alert for signs of enemy fire from the ground.

The helicopter and its crew are behind enemy lines on a medical evacuation mission. They touch down in a clearing. Two soldiers slide out of the forest carrying a third between them. Quickly, the medevac crew loads the wounded soldier onto a stretcher in the cabin of the helicopter.

As the copter rises from the ground and heads back to safety, the flight medic has already started to treat her patient's wounds.

Far and Away
When they're outfitted with extra fuel pods, Black Hawks can fly more than 1,100 miles.

The swept-back tips of the **rotor blades** help this helicopter fly faster and with less noise.

On a fast-moving helicopter, the tips of the rotor blades can be moving close to the speed of sound. That causes shock waves to build up in the air, creating noise and requiring more power from the engine. The shape of these blade tips helps reduce the shock waves.

Hail to the Chief

Another military chopper, the Sikorsky VH-3D, carries the president of the United States and is known as *Marine One*.

A Black Hawk's **cabin** can be set up in different ways. It can hold 11 soldiers with full gear, or up to 20 with light equipment. The seats can be taken out to turn the helicopter into an ambulance with space for up to six patients lying on stretchers.

The pilot and copilot of the U.S. Army's Black Hawk sit side by side in the **cockpit**. A third crew member rides in the cabin. Other helicopters have different crew sizes. The Army's Apache helicopter has a crew of two: a pilot who sits behind and a gunner who sits in front.

The **wire strike protection system (WSPS)** is a system of blades and deflectors that cuts through wires if the helicopter hits them.

This is necessary because helicopter pilots often fly very close to the ground to avoid being seen by the enemy. This strategy is called "nap-of-the-earth" flight.

A **refueling probe** lets the helicopter refuel from a tanker in midair.

The helicopter is built with **heavy armor** below to help defend it from ground fire.

Land and Sea Rescue

An essential part of the Coast Guard's search-and-rescue efforts is the type of helicopter known as a Dolphin, shown here. With their rescue hoists, slings, and baskets Dolphins can pluck sailors, swimmers, and downed aircraft pilots from the water and rush them to treatment.

RESCUE ON THE WAVES

A capsized fishing boat founders in the waves. Only its hull can be seen above the water. Nearby, a sailor bobs in his orange life jacket. The water is cold. Minutes count. The man can only survive for less than an hour before he will die of hypothermia.

An orange and white Coast Guard helicopter circles overhead. The pilot spots the man in the water and descends to hover 50 feet above him as he rises and falls with the ocean swells.

The helicopter's computerized controls keep it rock-steady as it hovers in the gusting wind. A steady downwash of air from the rotor sends a circle of spray across the surface of the water.

A rescue swimmer, wearing a life jacket, fins, and a snorkel, is lowered on the rescue hoist cable. She battles the waves, reaches the floating sailor, and buckles a sling around the man's body.

She gives a signal to the hoist engineer, and both swimmer and sailor rise from the water at the end of the hoist cable. The engineer helps them into the open door, and the helicopter heads for land.

Instead of a tail rotor, the Dolphin has an 11-bladed **fenestron** (FEN-uh-stron), or fan, in a hooded opening in its tail fin.

The **rescue hoist** can lift 600 pounds. Its cable is almost 300 feet long. In rough conditions or at night, the rescue swimmer is lowered on the cable. During daylight in calm seas, the swimmer jumps from the door of the aircraft into the water.

Air Ambulances

Helicopters like the Dolphin aren't used only for water rescues. They can serve as air ambulances for victims who need treatment right away, in which case the copters are often fitted with ambulance equipment. A version of the Dolphin helicopter pictured here can carry four patients on stretchers, two stacked on each side of the cabin like bunk beds. A doctor or paramedic rides along.

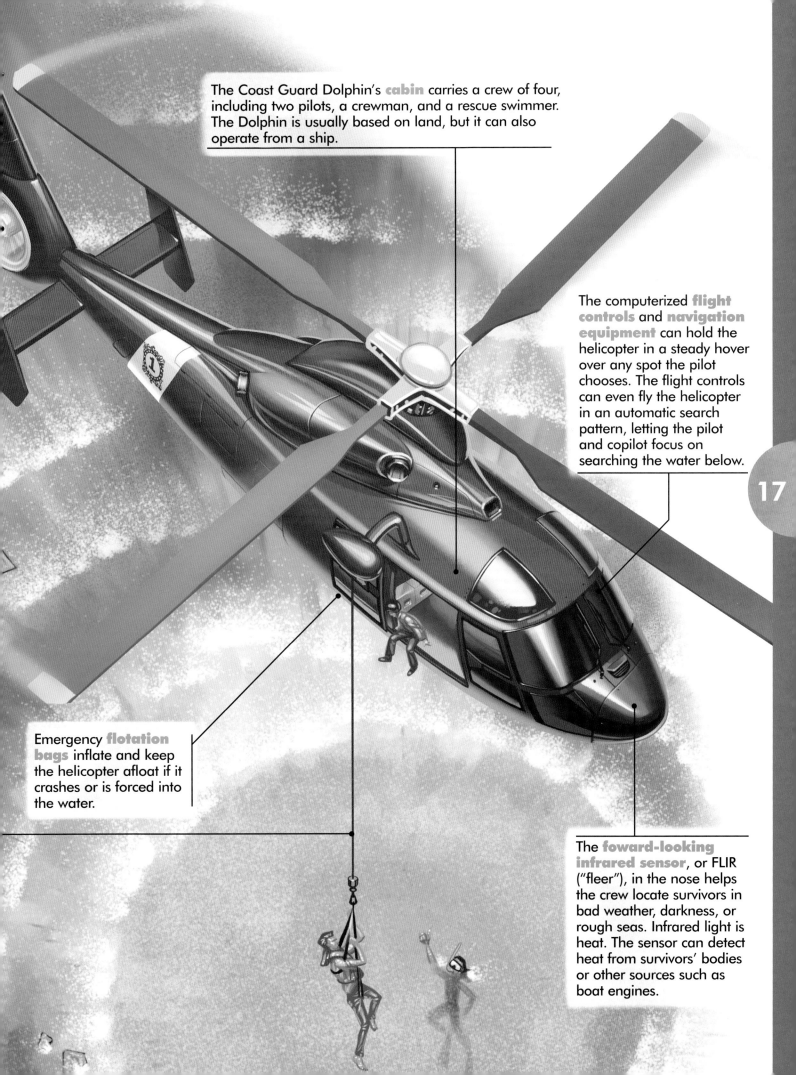

The Coast Guard Dolphin's **cabin** carries a crew of four, including two pilots, a crewman, and a rescue swimmer. The Dolphin is usually based on land, but it can also operate from a ship.

The computerized **flight controls** and **navigation equipment** can hold the helicopter in a steady hover over any spot the pilot chooses. The flight controls can even fly the helicopter in an automatic search pattern, letting the pilot and copilot focus on searching the water below.

Emergency **flotation bags** inflate and keep the helicopter afloat if it crashes or is forced into the water.

The **foward-looking infrared sensor**, or FLIR ("fleer"), in the nose helps the crew locate survivors in bad weather, darkness, or rough seas. Infrared light is heat. The sensor can detect heat from survivors' bodies or other sources such as boat engines.

Cop-ters

Pilots of police helicopters, like the MD500 shown here, can spot criminals who might otherwise be able to hide from officers on the ground. In a chase, the helicopter can follow a car anywhere without having to worry about traffic, bystanders, or turns in the road. The copters are fast, too—they can zoom ahead at 175 mph!

Different helicopters have different numbers of rotor blades.

Helicopters with more rotor blades generally make less noise than helicopters with fewer. This aircraft's five-bladed rotor helps make it quieter for use over cities.

CATCHING THE BAD GUYS

It's 2:00 a.m. The warehouse's alarm goes off. With screeching tires, a van pulls away from the loading dock carrying a million-dollar shipment of high-tech electronics!

Police cars rush toward the scene, but the officers know they'll be too late. The streets in the neighborhood are like a maze, full of twists, turns, and narrow alleys where the criminals can escape.

But the police helicopter is already in the air, flying a figure-eight patrol pattern over the city. The dispatcher radios the pilot, and in minutes the chopper is hovering over the warehouse district. The pilot switches on the powerful searchlight. The beam lights up the streets.

The van speeds up, but the helicopter has a perfect bird's-eye view of the streets from its perch high above. On the radio, the pilot guides the patrol cars on the ground. In moments the burglars' van is boxed in.

While the officers collar the criminals, the helicopter goes back to patrolling the city from the sky.

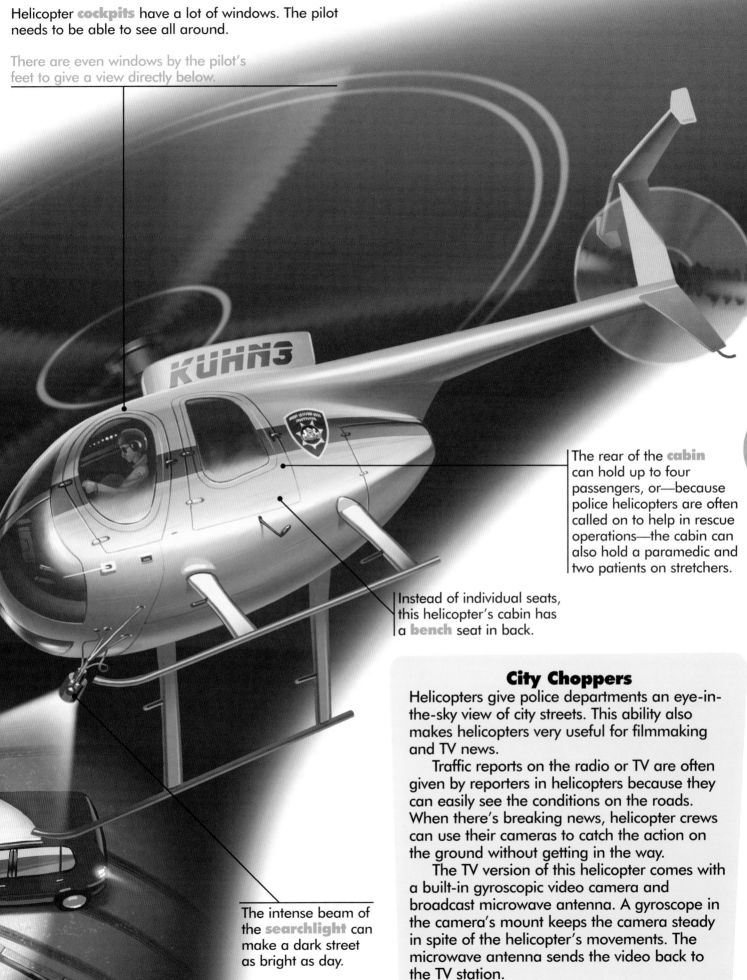

Helicopter **cockpits** have a lot of windows. The pilot needs to be able to see all around.

There are even windows by the pilot's feet to give a view directly below.

The rear of the **cabin** can hold up to four passengers, or—because police helicopters are often called on to help in rescue operations—the cabin can also hold a paramedic and two patients on stretchers.

Instead of individual seats, this helicopter's cabin has a **bench** seat in back.

The intense beam of the **searchlight** can make a dark street as bright as day.

City Choppers

Helicopters give police departments an eye-in-the-sky view of city streets. This ability also makes helicopters very useful for filmmaking and TV news.

Traffic reports on the radio or TV are often given by reporters in helicopters because they can easily see the conditions on the roads. When there's breaking news, helicopter crews can use their cameras to catch the action on the ground without getting in the way.

The TV version of this helicopter comes with a built-in gyroscopic video camera and broadcast microwave antenna. A gyroscope in the camera's mount keeps the camera steady in spite of the helicopter's movements. The microwave antenna sends the video back to the TV station.

Tiltrotor Craft

This combination airplane-helicopter is called an Osprey. It's a type of aircraft known as a tiltrotor. It has wings like an airplane and two large rotors like a helicopter. It takes off, lands, and hovers with lift from its rotors, like a helicopter. As soon as it gains enough forward speed for the wings to provide lift (about 120 mph), the engines tilt forward and the Osprey flies like an airplane.

Best of Both Worlds

The airplane crosses above the shoreline at a cruising speed of 300 mph toward open water. It's a stubby-looking aircraft, with engines at the very tips of its wings. In the cabin, a team of marines rides alongside a stretcher bearing an injured fighter pilot. The marines have plucked the pilot from enemy territory where his plane went down, 150 miles inland.

The droning sound of the propellers changes suddenly. The pilot has spotted their ship and has begun to slow the aircraft. As the plane slows down, the engines tilt upward until the propellers point straight into the air. The airplane has transformed itself into a helicopter! It stops in midair, hovering above the deck of the ship. The pilot lowers the aircraft slowly to the deck. Mission accomplished!

VTOL
VTOL stands for "vertical takeoff and landing." Because it's a VTOL aircraft, the Osprey can take off and land in a small space.

Engines pivot between pointing up and pointing forward.

The **refueling probe** lets the Osprey refuel in midair for longer missions.

Wings vs. Rotors
The amount of lift an airfoil provides depends on its surface area. Fixed-wing aircraft, with their larger wing surface creating less drag, are more efficient than helicopters. They can fly farther and faster. But fixed-wing aircraft need long runways or aircraft carriers. A tiltrotor aircraft combines the small space needs of a helicopter with the larger range and speed of an airplane.

Takes Off Like a Plane, Flies Like a Helicopter!

©Museum of Flight/CORBIS

This aircraft is an autogiro (aw-toe-JI-ro), or gyroplane. An autogiro has a propeller to move it forward, like an airplane. But instead of wings it has a rotor, like a helicopter.

As the propeller pulls the autogiro forward, air flows through the rotor and turns it like a windmill.

When the air turns the rotor fast enough, it creates lift and the autogiro flies into the air!

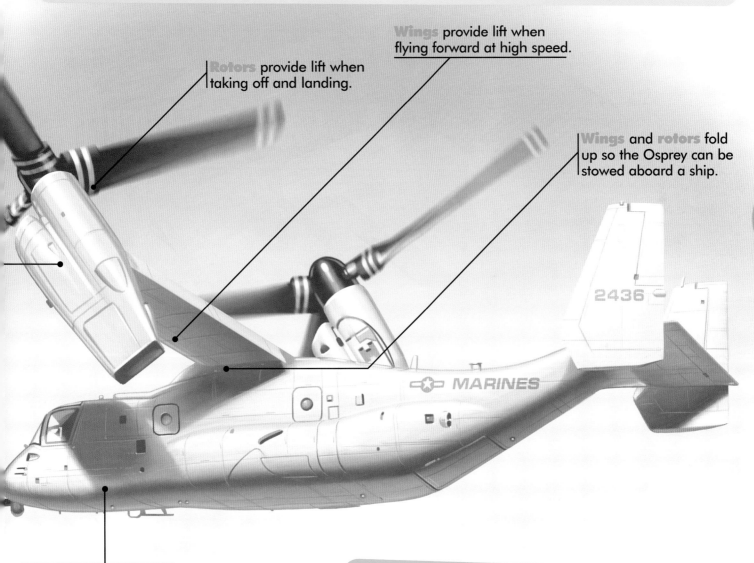

Rotors provide lift when taking off and landing.

Wings provide lift when flying forward at high speed.

Wings and **rotors** fold up so the Osprey can be stowed aboard a ship.

21

2436

MARINES

The **cabin** has seats for 24 in addition to the three-person crew.

Autorotation

If a helicopter flies downward, air flows upward through the rotor. Just as with an autogiro, this air can spin the rotor without the engine. It's called autorotation. All helicopters are built so the rotors can spin without the engine, much like the way your bike's wheels can spin when you're coasting. Using autorotation, a helicopter can get enough lift from its rotor to land safely even if the engine quits.

Ultralights

Ultralight helicopters are small, personal aircraft with a limited size, range, and speed. An ultralight helicopter can be built from a kit for a fraction of the price of a full-sized aircraft. Right now ultralights are only built and flown for recreation. But in the future, personal helicopters may be useful for all kinds of jobs, including wildlife research, pipeline and power line inspection, aerial photography, and many other activities.

WHALE WATCH

The marine biologist walks over to the tiny helicopter on the pebbled beach. She pulls her gloves and helmet on, climbs into the seat, and starts the engine. The twin-bladed rotor of the Mosquito spins to life. Buzzing like a giant bumblebee, the ultralight lifts from the ground, then rises diagonally into the air.

From a thousand feet up, the biologist looks down on the sparkling blue sea. Soon she spots a plume of mist rising from the water in a hidden cove. It's a pod of orcas. The biologist banks the helicopter in a wide turn. Here's what she's been looking for: an orca calf, born just a few days earlier. It's swimming beside its mother amid the other sleek, black-and-white bodies. The baby is healthy and doing well.

The biologist follows the pod and observes the whales from above as they swim around the narrow channels, bays, and inlets of the islands.

She keeps a careful eye on her fuel supply. After half an hour it's time to return.

The two-bladed **main rotor** measures less than 20 feet across.

The ultralight works like a regular helicopter: the **cyclic control** changes the pitch of the main rotor blades in a cycle, and that moves the helicopter in different directions.

Antitorque pedals are connected by cables to the tail rotor.

Flying without a License
Although safe piloting of an ultralight helicopter requires plenty of training and practice, no pilot's license is required. That's true if you plan on flying one in the U.S., at least. Laws in other countries can keep unlicensed pilots grounded.

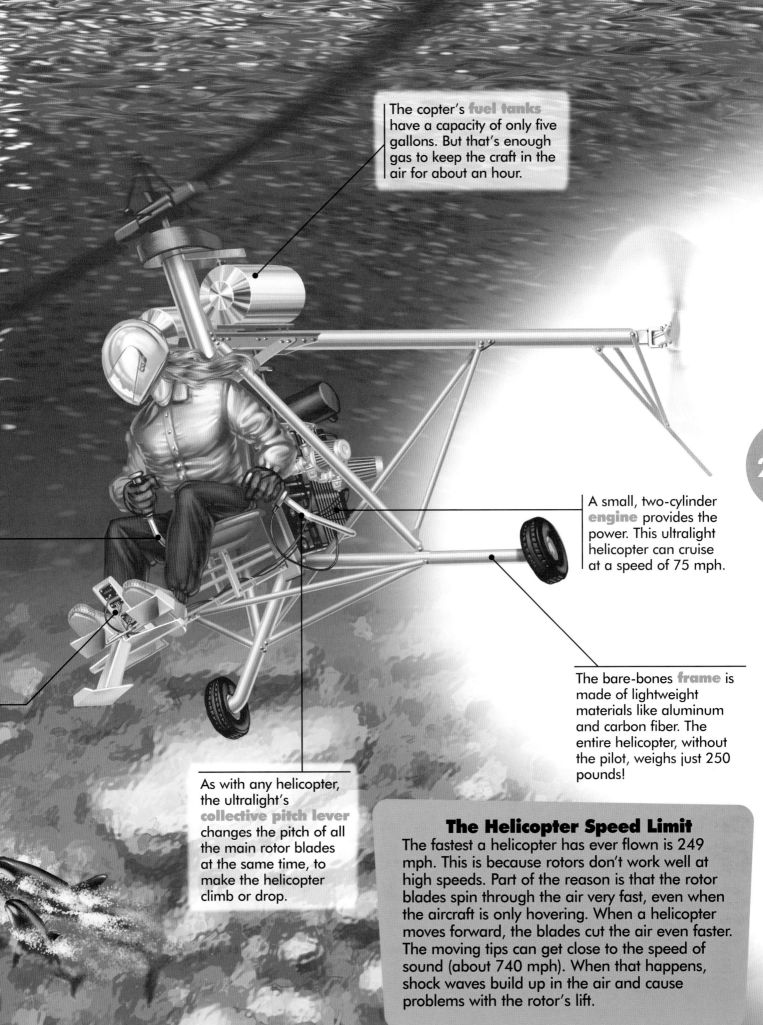

The copter's **fuel tanks** have a capacity of only five gallons. But that's enough gas to keep the craft in the air for about an hour.

A small, two-cylinder **engine** provides the power. This ultralight helicopter can cruise at a speed of 75 mph.

The bare-bones **frame** is made of lightweight materials like aluminum and carbon fiber. The entire helicopter, without the pilot, weighs just 250 pounds!

As with any helicopter, the ultralight's **collective pitch lever** changes the pitch of all the main rotor blades at the same time, to make the helicopter climb or drop.

The Helicopter Speed Limit

The fastest a helicopter has ever flown is 249 mph. This is because rotors don't work well at high speeds. Part of the reason is that the rotor blades spin through the air very fast, even when the aircraft is only hovering. When a helicopter moves forward, the blades cut the air even faster. The moving tips can get close to the speed of sound (about 740 mph). When that happens, shock waves build up in the air and cause problems with the rotor's lift.

History of Helicopters

ANCIENT HISTORY

In the fourth century A.D., 1,700 years ago, the Chinese scholar Ko Hung wrote about a flying machine powered by "blades" attached to leather straps. Ko Hung didn't say how the machine was supposed to fly, but some people believe he was describing a helicopter.

In the Middle Ages, children in Europe played with a toy called a "Chinese top." It was a stick with blades at the top (shown at right above). When you pulled its string, it flew into the air. This toy might look familiar to you. Kids today still have them!

More than 500 years ago, around the year 1480, the Italian artist, architect, scientist, and engineer Leonardo da Vinci drew an idea for a rotating wing shaped like a large screw (shown at right). He called it a helixpteron, from the Greek words for "spiral wing." The same Greek words are combined in our word helicopter.

Leonardo thought his canvas air screw could be used in a human-powered flying machine. He didn't realize that humans don't have enough muscle power to lift their own weight into the air with a machine like this.

EARLY HELICOPTERS

The famous inventor Thomas Edison tried his hand at helicopter design. In the 1880s he experimented with a helicopter with a motor powered by gun cotton, a very flammable material used in guns and cannons. After nearly blowing up his lab, his assistants, and himself, Edison gave up.

In 1907, almost four years after the Wright brothers' first airplane flight, a French inventor named Paul Cornu made the world's first vertical free flight in a helicopter. Cornu's machine (shown at left) carried him a few feet into the air and stayed aloft for several seconds.

©Bettmann/CORBIS

IGOR SIKORSKY

The most influential helicopter inventor was Russian-born Igor Sikorsky. Sikorsky experimented with aircraft as a young man and even tried making some helicopters. They didn't work well, and Sikorsky spent many years building airplanes instead.

He moved to the United States in 1919 and eventually started his own airplane company. When he invented his first working helicopter in 1939, helicopters became really popular.

Sikorsky flew his experimental vehicles himself. Outside, he almost always wore a fedora hat. Over the years, a legend grew that any pilot who wore Sikorsky's hat, even for a few seconds, would never be hurt while flying a helicopter.

Sikorsky thought that by the 1950s or 1960s, people all over the world might have their own helicopters. That prediction didn't come true, but he did help turn the helicopter into the common and useful machine it is today.

Igor Sikorsky died in 1972, but his company still makes helicopters.

Imaginary Flying Machines

Many artists and writers imagined flying machines that worked like helicopters. In 1876 the French science-fiction author Jules Verne wrote a book called *The Clipper of the Clouds*. The clipper in the story was an airship called the *Albatross*. The *Albatross* looked like a sailing ship. In the story it was held in the air by 74 helicopter-like rotors, powered by electricity.

Coming Up

What's next for helicopters? Here are some recent and future design ideas.

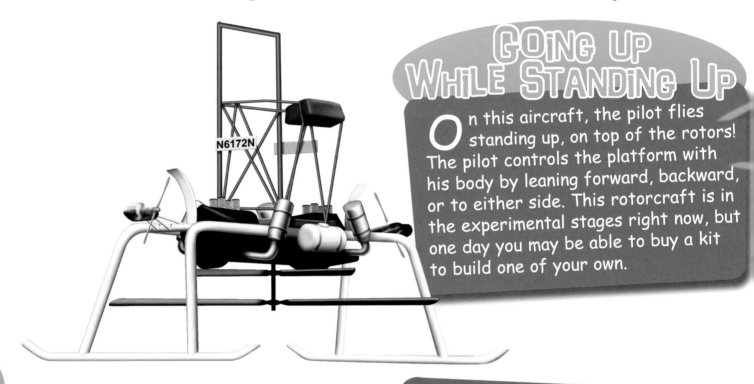

GOING UP WHILE STANDING UP

On this aircraft, the pilot flies standing up, on top of the rotors! The pilot controls the platform with his body by leaning forward, backward, or to either side. This rotorcraft is in the experimental stages right now, but one day you may be able to buy a kit to build one of your own.

IS IT A FLYING SAUCER?

No, it's a tiltrotor aircraft called the Humming. The Humming's rotor is a giant ring around the outside of its airplanelike body. This aircraft is still being designed.

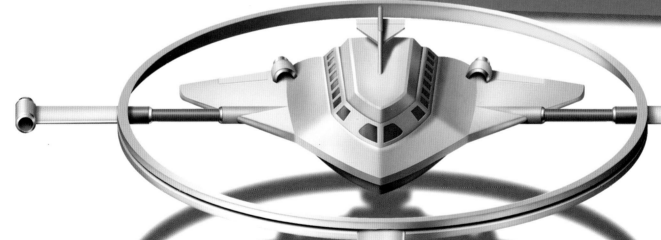

- The four rotor blades are short and wide. They stick out from the spinning ring.
- The aircraft will have jet or rocket engines around the outside of the ring to turn the rotor for takeoff.
- Depending on the design, the Humming may have jet engines at the back to propel it once it is in the air. For takeoff, the rotor is flat.
- The Humming takes off and lands like a helicopter, so it can use a small landing space.
- Once airborne, the rotor ring tilts to a vertical flight position and the aircraft flies like an airplane.

WHERE'S THE TAIL ROTOR?

This helicopter doesn't have one! It's a recent helicopter design called NOTAR, which stands for "no tail rotor." Instead, the helicopter's jet engine forces air to go spinning along the inside of the tail boom. The air is pushed out of slots in the boom.

Remember the Coanda effect? (Air flowing over a curved surface follows the curve.) The high-speed air flowing out of the slots follows the curve of the tail boom. In the same way that air flowing over a curved airfoil creates lift, air flowing around the side of the tail boom creates a sideways force. The sideways force acts against torque from the main rotor, just like a normal tail rotor does.

NOTAR helicopters are much quieter than helicopters with tail rotors, so they can fly and land in places like cities without bothering people. They also prevent accidents from damaged tail rotors, or the serious or fatal injuries that can happen if a careless person walks into the moving tail rotor of a helicopter on the ground.

This experimental aircraft is the Dragonfly Canard Rotor Wing. (A canard is a short stabilizer at the front of an aircraft.) The rotor wing is on top. It spins around like a rotor to let the Dragonfly take off and land like a helicopter. After takeoff, the rotor locks in place and becomes a wing, and the aircraft flies like an airplane.

The Dragonfly is being developed for the military as an unmanned aerial vehicle, or UAV. These are robotic aircraft, so they can be sent on missions into enemy territory without endangering a pilot or other human crew. They're small, so they're hard to detect. The Dragonfly is only 18 feet long, about the size of an ultralight helicopter's rotor disk.

ROBO COPTER

Assembly Instructions

The parts included in your Flight Test Lab:

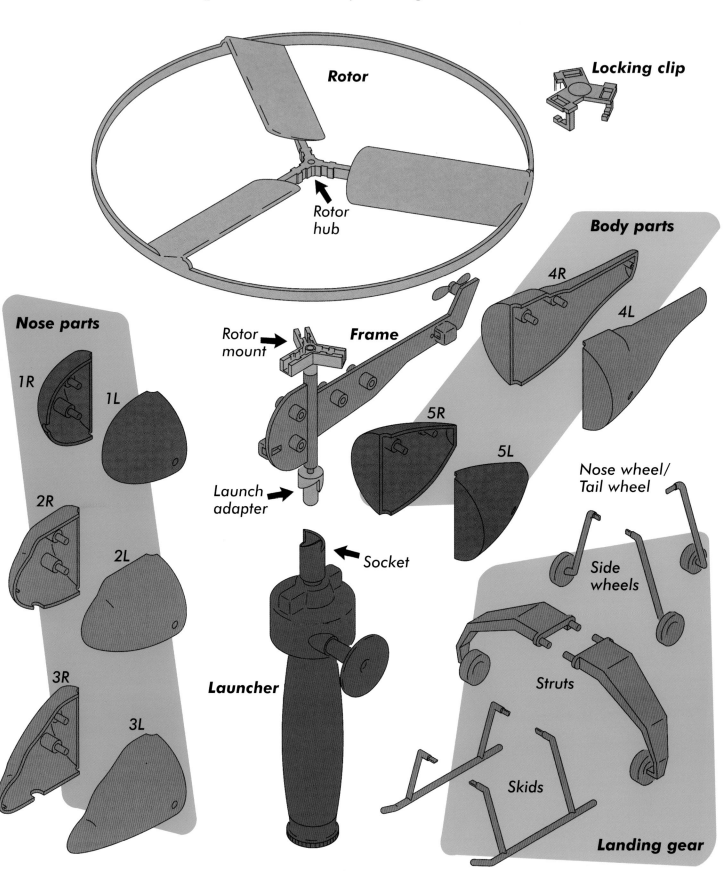

Rotor

Locking clip

Rotor hub

Body parts

4R

4L

Nose parts

Rotor mount

Frame

1R

1L

5R

5L

2R

Launch adapter

2L

Nose wheel/ Tail wheel

Socket

Side wheels

3R

Launcher

3L

Struts

Skids

Landing gear

These steps show you how to assemble the Dolphin, but the steps for building any helicopter are very similar.

Step 1
Insert the nose wheel into the square hole in the front of the frame.

Step 2
Snap the right and left halves of the nose (parts 3R and 3L) onto the frame. The part numbers are inside the pieces and the left and right sides of the frame are marked. Squeeze the two halves of the nose together until they snap tight.

Step 3
Snap the right and left halves of the body (parts 4R and 4L) onto the frame.

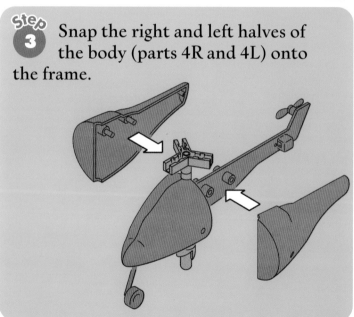

Step 4
Insert the side wheels, one on the right side and one on the left side, into the holes near the bottom of the body.

29

Step 5
Fit the rotor hub in the rotor mount on the frame. The gusset braces should be on the underside of the rotor. Make sure the rotor fits into the rotor mount snugly.

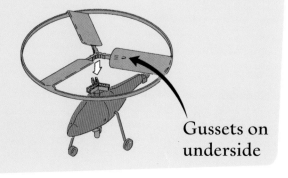

Gussets on underside

Step 6
Set the locking clip over the rotor hub and rotor mount. Next, turn the clip clockwise to lock the rotor in place.

To remove the locking clip, gently pry the little arms from the rotor hub and turn the clip counterclockwise.

With your Flight Test Lab you can assemble the four helicopters shown below. (The rotors are drawn transparent so you can see all the parts.) The illustrations lay out the parts you'll need for assembling each copter. Once you've built them all, you can mix noses, bodies, and landing gear to create your own designs. At first, the parts will fit very tightly and will be hard to put together and take apart. The more you use them, the easier this will be.

DOLPHIN

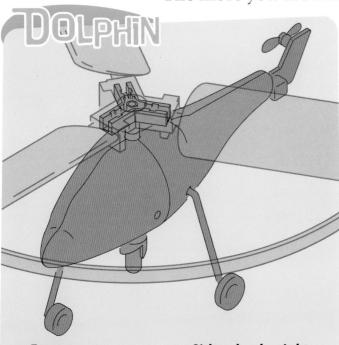

- Frame
- Nose wheel
- Nose, right and left (3R and 3L)
- Body, right and left (4R and 4L)
- Side wheels, right and left
- Rotor
- Locking clip

HELITANKER

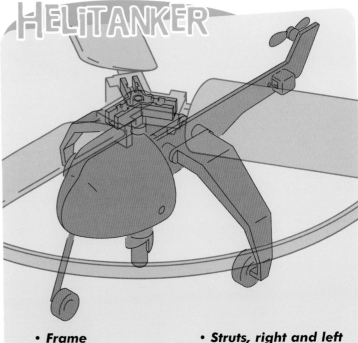

- Frame
- Nose wheel
- Nose, right and left (2R and 2L)
- Struts, right and left
- Rotor
- Locking clip

MD500

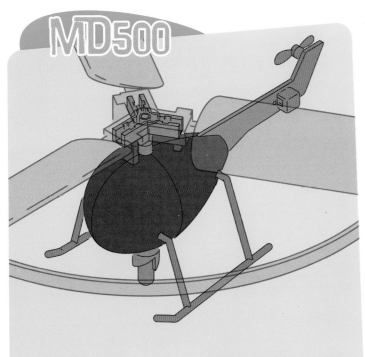

- Frame
- Nose, right and left (1R and 1L)
- Body, right and left (5R and 5L)
- Skids, right and left
- Rotor
- Locking clip

BLACK HAWK

- Frame
- Nose, right and left (3R and 3L)
- Body, right and left (4R and 4L)
- Tail wheel
- Side wheels, right and left
- Rotor
- Locking clip

Launching

Launching helicopters with the power launcher is easy.

Step 1

Insert the launch adapter into the socket.

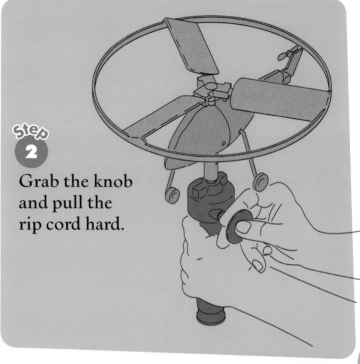

Step 2

Grab the knob and pull the rip cord hard.

Tip

Just as a helicopter pilot changes course by changing where the rotor shaft points, you can launch your helicopter in different directions.

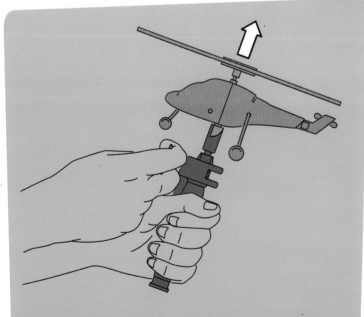

To launch a copter ahead of you, point the power launcher forward at an angle.

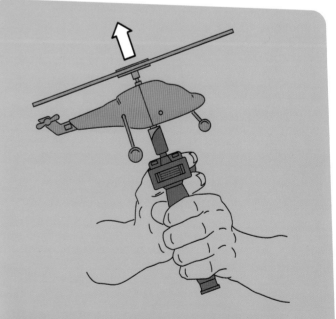

To launch a copter to the side, point the power launcher where you want the copter to go.

These helicopters are for outdoor play only. Watch for obstacles when you launch your copters. Launch them away from trees, walls, roofs, etc. And never point them at anyone.

Glossary
of Important Helicopter Terms

Airfoil
A structure, like an airplane wing or helicopter rotor blade, that creates lift when it moves through the air.

Angle of attack
The angle between an airfoil and the direction it is traveling through the air.

Antitorque rotor
The rotor on a helicopter's tail that keeps the aircraft from spinning due to torque from the main rotor. Changes the direction the helicopter is pointing. Also called the tail rotor.

Autogiro
A rotorcraft on which the rotor is turned by air pressure while a propeller pulls the craft forward. Also called a gyroplane.

Collective pitch lever
The helicopter control that changes the pitch of all rotor blades at the same time. Moves the helicopter up and down.

Cyclic control
The helicopter control that changes the pitch of each rotor blade individually as the rotor turns. Steers the helicopter.

Drag
Air resistance. The force that acts against thrust to slow an aircraft down.

Fuselage
The body of a helicopter or airplane.

Helicopter
A rotorcraft that gets all of its lift from a power-driven rotor or rotors.

Lift
The force that acts against gravity to raise an aircraft into the air and keep it there.

Nap-of-the-earth
The kind of flying where the pilot flies the helicopter close to the ground, following the rising and falling contours of the land.

Pitch
The angle between a rotor blade and the circle of the rotor hub, sometimes called the pitch angle. Also, the front-to-back rocking movement of an aircraft.

Roll
Side-to-side rocking movement of an aircraft.

Rotor
A set of rotating or spinning airfoils.

Rotor blade
An individual airfoil. Part of a rotor.

Rotor disk
The circle created by a spinning rotor.

Rotorcraft
An aircraft that gets lift from a rotor or rotors.

Swash plate
The part of the rotor that controls the cyclic pitch of the rotor blades.

Thrust
The force that acts against drag to move an aircraft through the air.

Torque
Twisting force.

Yaw
Side-to-side swiveling motion of an aircraft.